The Gryphon Press

—a voice for the voiceless—

These books are dedicated to those who foster compassion toward all animals.

Jeannie Houdini is dedicated to our small animal friends, all of whom require tender care.
—Mary-Ann Stouck

With thanks to Kaia Lunde and Coralin Evans for their artwork.
—Rebecca Evans

Copyright © 2019 text by Mary-Ann Stouck
Copyright © 2019 art by Rebecca Evans

Text set in Georgia by Bookmobile Design & Digital Publisher Services
Printed in Canada

Library of Congress Cataloging-in-Publication Data
CIP date is on file with the Library of Congress.

ISBN: 978-0-940719-40-8

1 3 5 7 9 10 8 6 4 2

I am the voice of the voiceless:
Through me, the dumb shall speak;
Till the deaf world's ear be made to hear
The cry of the wordless weak.

—from a poem by Ella Wheeler Wilcox, early 20th-century poet

JEANNIE HOUDINI

A Hamster's Tale

Written by Mary-Ann Stouck

Illustrated by Rebecca Evans

Jeannie the hamster lived in a tiny house.
Her bedroom was a coconut shell with a hole for a doorway.
Her cage had a red plastic wheel, a seed dish, and a water bottle.

Jeannie slept during most of the day, and when she woke up in the
evening, she almost never used her plastic wheel, because
however fast she ran on it, she never got anywhere different.

Once a week, the twins' mother said to Mateo and Martina, "It's time to wash your hands and clean Jeannie's cage."

Then Mateo and Martina each said to one another, "It's *your* turn."

"No fighting," said their mother. "And remember to wash your hands afterward too!"

Although the twins had chosen Jeannie for a pet, they soon lost interest in her. Sometimes they forgot to refill her water bottle and did not notice when her seed dish was empty.

Nobody asked Sophia to care for Jeannie.
She sometimes felt left out and lonely.

When the twins cleaned Jeannie's cage, they lined the bottom with soft bedding and fresh newspaper. Some weeks it was the section with real estate ads. Martina read these out loud:

"Magnificent Mansion for Sale! Gigantic Kitchen! Humongous Rooms!"

"Just like my dollhouse," thought Sophia.

HOUDINI
GREATEST ESCAPE
ARTIST EVER!

Houdini was born in Hungary One of his public challenges
in 1874, the son of Rabbi Mayer of long standing that he could
Samuel Weiss. duplicate or expose an
As an outstanding personage seemingly magic feat we
of the American stage, his accepted by Ramen B
popularity lasted for a Egyptian mystifier, in Aug
quarter-century. Beginning The Egyptian has creat
his stage career as a trapeze sensation by remaining
performer, he toured the sealed coffin under w
world. Houdini counted among nineteen minutes.
his audiences the royalty of breaths and conse
Europe and Asia. He wrote oxygen did it,"
numerous treatises intended to who entered
fraud. His book, "A stayed the
Among the Spirits," Houdi
furor amon

One day, when the twins were lining Jeannie's cage, Martina read a different
kind of headline: "HOUDINI—GREATEST ESCAPE ARTIST EVER!"

Their mother said, "Houdini was a magician who could always escape.
Even when he was tied up inside a wooden box that was dropped into the sea,
Houdini still escaped."

That night, the twins forgot to shut Jeannie's cage door.
The next morning, the cage was empty.

"Jeannie escaped!" Sophia said when she came down for breakfast.

"Would you look for Jeannie?" her mother asked.

Sophia looked everywhere. At last she found Jeannie in a corner of the hall, nibbling a few cracker crumbs.

Sophia picked Jeannie up, careful not to squeeze her. Gently, she stroked Jeannie's soft fur before she brought her back to her cage, making sure to shut the cage door. Then she washed her hands and sat down to breakfast.

The very next morning, Jeannie disappeared again. Sophia found her halfway up the stairs.

"How did you get out?" Sophia asked Jeannie.

"Maybe she's Jeannie Houdini," Sophia's mother said, laughing.

Sophia looked carefully at Jeannie's cage and saw a small opening in the bars next to the plastic tray.

Sophia stuffed the space with a piece of cardboard. She did not know that hamsters could nibble through paper and even cardboard.

The next morning, Jeannie was asleep in her coconut bed. Sophia did not disturb her.

That evening, Sophia played with her dollhouse. The living room had a sofa and a tiny light that turned on and off. The kitchen had strawberry-pink cupboards, and upstairs there were four bedrooms. It was, in fact, a Magnificent Mansion.

When Sophia woke up the next morning,
she noticed something different about the dollhouse.
A lamp had fallen over, and the sofa was tipped backward.

She looked more closely.

Behind the dollhouse couch was a furry brown-and-white ball.
It was Jeannie.

"Oh Jeannie," whispered Sophia. "How did you get into my dollhouse? You must be bored in your cage. That's why you keep escaping!"

Sophia picked Jeannie up, careful not to startle her or squeeze her. Downstairs, she gave Jeannie her breakfast of strawberries and sunflower seeds.

After that, every day before Sophia went to school, she fed Jeannie.

She made sure that there was no opening in Jeannie's cage large enough for a daring escape.

Every evening, Sophia and Jeannie played.

Jeannie ran up and down the dollhouse stairs.

She sniffed in all the corners.

And she nibbled sunflower tidbits in the dollhouse kitchen.

Every week, without being reminded, Sophia cleaned Jeannie's cage, washing her hands carefully each time. Every day, she refilled Jeannie's water bottle and seed dish. Every day, they played together.

Jeannie was no longer bored. Sophia was no longer lonely. They were the best of friends.

How to Have a Happy Hamster

If you are thinking of getting a hamster for a pet, adopt rather than buy. Check with your local shelter or animal rescue group for hamsters already waiting for good homes. More than anything, it's important to know what will make your pet happy. A hamster is small and easily frightened, requiring careful handling, especially at the beginning. Hamsters are best suited as pets for older children who are able to take into account their unique needs and to respect that most of their activity takes place at night.

CARING FOR YOUR HAMSTER

Hamsters need to be housed by themselves, but they also need stimulation. Apart from daily changes of food and water, their cage should contain clean bedding (no wood-based, corn-cob, sawdust, or clay cat litter products) and an assortment of fun stuff, such as tunnels, ladders, and wheels. Appropriate chew toys for your hamster to gnaw on are vital so that her teeth don't get overgrown, as overgrown teeth prevent hamsters from being able to eat.

MAKING FRIENDS WITH YOUR HAMSTER

After your hamster has started exploring her new surroundings, which may take several days, you can begin to bond. Offer treats such as nuts and small pieces of vegetable and fruit; research which ones are safe for hamsters. Let your hamster take treats from your fingers. As your hamster gets used to you, encourage her to climb onto your hand for a treat. This process helps accustom the hamster to your scent before you try to pick her up. Repeat this process for several short sessions daily. Hamsters have keen hearing, so quiet, soothing talk helps them get used to your presence. When your hamster seems ready to be picked up, do so by cupping her in both hands (without squeezing!), and remember to support her body so she feels secure.

CLEANLINESS

Hamsters are cuddly little creatures, but they can also carry salmonella—intestinal bacteria that may cause sickness in adults and children. Therefore, it is important to wash your hands both before and after playing with your hamster or cleaning her cage. Hamsters hoard their food in their cheek pouches and in their nests, so cage cleaning should include changing their bedding and removing uneaten food.

FURTHER RESOURCES

There are many helpful resources online to assist you with caring for your hamster. Here are a few to get you started:

www.humanesociety.org/resources/hamster-right-pet-you

www.petmd.com/exotic/care/evr_ex_hm_how-to-care-for-your-hamster

www.mnpocketpetrescue.org/hamsters

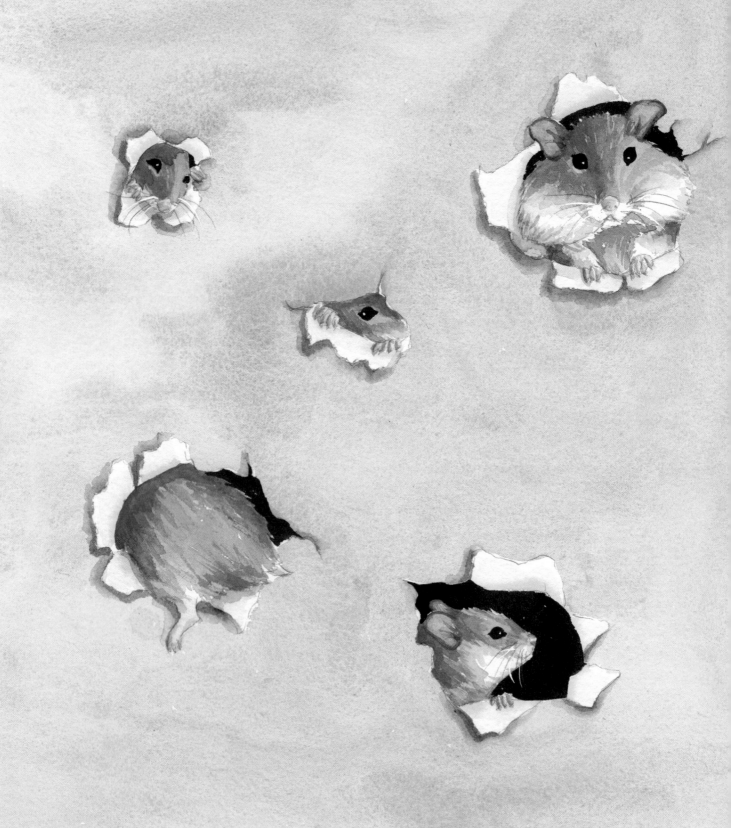